D1714435

MOSCARDINO

by Enrico Pea

translated from the Italian by Ezra Pound

archipelago books

Copyright © 2005 Archipelago Books

First Edition

All rights reserved. No part of this book may be reproduced or transmitted
in any form without the prior written permission of the publisher

Library of Congress Cataloging-in-Publication Data
Pea, Enrico, 1881–1958.
[Moscardino. English]
Moscardino / Enrico Pea ; translated from the Italian by Ezra Pound. — 1st ed.
p. cm.
ISBN 0-9749680-3-X
I. Pound, Ezra, 1885–1972. II. Title.
PQ4835.E22M6313 2005
853'.912 — dc22
2004020751

Archipelago Books
25 Jay Street, #203
Brooklyn, NY 11201
www.archipelagobooks.org

Distributed by Consortium Book Sales and Distribution
1045 Westgate Drive
St. Paul, MN 55114
www.cbsd.com

Moscardino
Copyright © 1955 by New Directions

All rights reserved

Cover art: Modigliani, Amedeo. *The Little Peasant*, ca. 1918. Oil on canvas.
Photo Credit: Tate Gallery, London / Art Resource, NY

This publication is made possible with public funds from the
New York State Council on the Arts, a State agency.

NYSCA

Contents

EP/EP: Ezra Pound — Enrico Pea

I think it's fair to say that Ezra Pound preferred novelists who at heart were poets. As for contemporary Italian writers, he was mainly interested in prose flavored by the earth: speech he heard from peasants, descriptions of people he met in the street; irrational, violent, yet wise characters mostly, as we find them in Tozzi and in Enrico Pea. Nothing abstract. E.P. and E.P. have both left us vivid descriptions of each other and their meetings, so we need not embroider.

I remember well the enthusiasm with which my father encouraged me to translate Thomas Hardy's *Under the Greenwood Tree*. He said he had met the best Italian writer and that as soon as I had a presentable chapter typed up, he would show the manuscript to him, because his opinion would count more than his own and he might have some good advice. Pound had already obtained Pea's permission to translate *Moscardino*, but he did not know who owned Hardy's copyright, or how one might secure it. However, the main thing was to get the job done, almost like running a race, as well as to learn the profession since I could not go to school. (In 1941, I had to leave school because of the war.)

The humility and the gentleness, the fun and the efficiency of Pound's behavior in his family circle is too often overshadowed by his public imperatives and even more so by the misreadings of outsiders. He knew that my language skills were insufficient for the task, just as he knew that there was no chance of getting his own translation published with the war going on.

In his first letter to Pea he addresses him as colleague:

Egregio Collega —

If you have no better offer, I ask permission to translate *Moscardino* into English. I am almost convinced of the impossibility of finding a publisher either in England or in the USA, but the book interests me and I am ready to give it a try.

The logistic problems seem to me purely theoretical, nevertheless I would like to know your feelings about it. I don't foresee a lucrative business either for author or translator. *Mah!*

Anyway, accept my sentiments, etc. I did not know that narrative art had reached Italy . . .

Cordialissimi saluti . . .

In general I have believed that the earnings should, if any there be, go approximately ¾ to the author and ¼ to the translator.

Pea answered promptly on June 13, 1941:

Caro amico —
You will have noticed that my work presents some difficulties
also because of certain idiomatic words and ways of speaking in
Versilia. Nevertheless I am glad for the request you make because *Moscardino* can be translated only by a man with a lively
and modern spirit like yourself.[. . .]

And thus the work began and, in time, I learned a new word: *redola*,
etymology uncertain, which I had never heard from my Italian teacher
in Florence, but which fits Hardy's "lane," in disaccord with the general terms in the dictionary. One of my most cherished typescripts
remains that first chapter with penned corrections by E.P. and E.P. At
sixteen it held promises of future glory. Now I can laugh about the
absolute inadequacy of my translation, which of course was never fit
to be published. But the awareness of how deeply concerned Pound
was not only with good writing, but also with my education, moves
me deeply.

It was thanks to the publisher, Vanni Scheiwiller, that Enrico Pea
wrote his "*grazie,* Ezra Pound" for *STAGIONE,* 1955, a number ded-
icated to Ezra Pound on his seventieth birthday, with contributions

solicited from the best Italian writers, who were concerned about Pound's detention at Saint Elisabeth's, from Accrocca and Anceschi to Bartoolini, Bertolucci, Betocchi, Bigongiari, Caproni, Carrieri, Fallacara, Giudici, Guidacci, Jahier, Luzi, Montale, Prampolini, Prezzolini, Quasimodo, Sereni, Soffici, Spaziani, Traverso, and Valeri. Scheiwiller himself, in his editorial, quoted Giovanni Papini's appeal on Pound's behalf to the American ambassador, Mrs. Luce, adding another string of names. It would seem that the Italian writers cared more about the poet's fate than his compatriots.

Vanni was barely twenty at the time (he was born in 1934) and had already published Pound's *Lavoro ed Usura* (1954), *Tre Cantos* (1954), and *Confucio: Studio Integrale e L'Asse che non vacilla* (1955). He then, with some difficulty, got permission from Pound's U.S. publisher, James Laughlin of New Directions, at Pound's instigation, to publish *Moscardino* in 1956; Pea's text, translated by John Drummond, served as introduction. The little volume was printed by the prince of printers, Giovanni Mardersteig, at his Stamperia Valdonega in Verona in one thousand copies of which perhaps one hundred were sold. Pound's own record had to be "aired" on October 26, 1941, under the title "Books and Music":

So a few weeks ago Monotti sez: ever read Pea's *Moscardino?* So I read it, and for the first time in your colloquitor's life he wuz tempted to TRANSLATE a novel, and did so. Ten years ago I had seen Enrico Pea passin' along the sea front and Gino [Saviotti] sez: It's a novelist. Having seen and known POLLEN IDEN, some hundreds, or probably thousands I was not interested in its being a novelist. But the book must be good or I wouldn't be more convinced of the fact AFTER having translated it, than I was before. Of course my act was impractical so far as you are concerned. I haven't the ghost of an idea how I am going to get the manuscript to America or get it published. Pea has never made a cent out of the original. Well neither had Joyce nor Eliot when I started trying to git someone to print 'em.

What's it like? Well, if Tom Hardy had been born a lot later, and lived in the hills up back the Lunigiana, which is down along the coast here, and if Hardy hadn't writ what ole Fordie used to call that "sort of small town paper journalese." And if a lot of other things, includin' temperament, had been different, and so forth . . . that might have been something like Pea's writin'—which I repeat is good writing — and was back in 1921 when *Moscardino* was printed. *Moscardino* is the name of the kid who is tellin' about his grandpop, a nickname like Buck.

As soon as the barriers are down I shall be sendin' a copy along for the enlightenment of the American public.

In the meantime, if anyone wants to learn how to write

Italian let 'em read the first chapter of *Forastiero* [*Il forestiero*, Firenze 1937] or the couple of pages on the bloke who had been twenty years in jail. This is just announcin' that Italy has a writer, and it is some time since I told anybody that ANY country on earth had a writer. Like Confucius, knocked 'round and done all sorts of jobs. Writes like a man who could make a good piece of mahogany furniture.

That furniture got immortalized in Canto 80:

> [. . .]
> reminding me of the Bank of Egypt
> and the gold bars
> in old Menelik's palace and the mahogany counters
> and desk work in the branch in, was it, Alexandria
> put there by Pea (Enrico)
> [. . .]

In Pisa, Pound must have remembered his conversations with Pea. Perhaps he had, at the time, encouraged him to write about his life in Egypt. *Vita in Egitto* was published in 1949.

I don't know what other books by Pea Pound read at Saint Elisabeth's. There's an amusing letter in which Pound informs Pea that "William Rufus, King of England, *un fiol di canass* (son of a bitch), used to swear by the 'volto sacro di Lucca.' Can you tell me if the famous crucifix is still in Lucca? Vultus Sanctus, 'scolpito da Nicedemo.' I don't know at the moment if I can use it, but perhaps there are some jokes or some local anecdote, like that donkey in Verona about which the Rev. Cav. Dott. Alesssandrro RRRobertson of the Scotch Church in Venice got so excited."

The Reverend Robertson is mentioned in Canto 76:

> [. . .]
> "Dawnt let 'em git you" burred the bearded Dottore
> when was the Scotch Kirrk in Venice
> to warn one against Babylonian intrigue
> [. . .]

And the statue of the donkey with ancient rituals still exists in Verona, as does the "Volto Santo" in Lucca. But the translation of the entire text of *Il romanzo di Moscardino* which includes *Il Volto Santo-Magometto-Il Servitore del Diavolo*, 1944, is still unpublished, although it was Pea's ardent wish to have it appear in English. Olga Rudge and John Drummond worked on it for several years, but I suppose the manuscript, unsolicited or rejected, like my Hardy translation, never reached the finished stage.

Pea's last letter to Pound at Saint Elisabeth's is dated March 26, 1958:

> *Mio carissimo* Pound,
>
> The Italian radio t-day, March 26, 1 o'clock, has announced that the American government has finally expressed the good intention to set you free. *Questa notizia ha messo in allegria la mia casa.* [. . .]

The joyful reunion, looked forward to, never took place. On August 11, 1958, Pea died. On that very day, we had addressed a card to the usual Bar Roma, Forte dei Marmi: "EZP *a* E.P. *salutissimi.*"

In 1981, for Pea's centenary, the province of Lucca sponsored a beautiful volume: *il mondo di Pea.* Pea's world: richly illustrated and with many interesting articles by his friends. On pp. 118–19, right above Montale's words ". . . The superb result is not surprising," we find the reproduction of the Pesce d'Oro, 1956 cover of *Moscardino*, and a photograph of Ezra Pound, who had died in 1972. Whether a consequence of remarkable editing and layout or of chance, the two friends would have liked it.

Mary de Rachewiltz
Brunnenburg, May 2004

Preface

Before the war Ezra Pound was no more than a name to me. Later I was to learn from Luigi Berti, then his authorized translator, something of the nature of his poetry, with its sudden interpolations of reminiscences, at times parenthetically incorporated in the rhythm of the song, at times abruptly detached from it.

"Ezra Pound is the mysterious master of the best of our modern poets, as he was in the past of Eliot, and of many others in England, France, and America. His poetry is a poetry of imagery, and often of analogy: the word has significance in itself even if it is not always immediately clear how its ordinary meaning is to be understood in the context . . ."

At the same time my curiosity began to be aroused by what I kept hearing of the man and his art. Giovanni Macchia, who was then teaching at the University of Pisa, spoke to me about him; so did G. B. Vicari, Leonardo Sinisgalli, and others. And with surprising simultaneity I also came across specimens of his poetry and repeated references to his name in print. "It happens like that," Sinisgalli explained to me: he was always prepared to see the working of occult forces in everything.

"It happens like that with ideas, discoveries, and inventions even with words: at a certain moment they begin to vibrate in the air, and will even cross the ocean in search of an ear tuned to receive them.

"A few days ago, in fact (I've no idea for what strange symbolic reason), a word I'd never heard of before came under my eyes at least five times in the space of a week. I almost felt I was being persecuted by what seemed to me a diabolic word: nassa. Never before had I even heard the sound of it, though I now know that it's the name for a kind of cigar-shaped, basket-work trap, made of canes or osiers, used for catching fish."

It was not long afterward, on reading an interview dealing with the American poet's opinion of various Italian writers, that I learned that Pound considered me one of the few worthy of being made known abroad.

War was already raging.

In a short and unexpected letter Pound had informed me of his proposal to translate *Moscardino*. It was typical of his dynamic personality that the next thing I knew (almost before he could have received my reply to his letter, which had certainly flattered my self-esteem) was the sight of him in person, jumping down from a cab, at the entrance to the café near the mole at Viareggio, where I used to work.

The first manifestations of fellow-feeling, like those of love, are nearly always mutual. And the exchange of a few words between Pound and myself, on the threshold of that café, established in an instant a perfect understanding. The physical appearance of the man attracted me immediately. I admired his air of civility, and it hardly seemed that his imposing figure, at once primitive and refined, carried the weight of more than fifty years. His bearing was lively; he was dressed with apparent negligence, but actually in clothes of sober good taste. The original pale copper of his somewhat disheveled hair was mingled with the grey due to his years. And the beard, though it covered his chin but sparsely, gave length to his slightly Mephistophelean features.

He would not let me take the brown case that swayed in his left hand. Inside the café, when he opened it on the marble-topped table, the half-moon of a typewriter's bars made its appearance. The metal clips held a sheet of paper on the roller, and on it were already listed words in the Versilia dialect that occurred in *Moscardino*.

On these we set to work immediately. As I explained their meaning, Pound typed the English equivalent beside each word. Then we got to talking about Egypt, whereupon I realized over what a wide field Pound's thirst for knowledge ranged. He was by no means satisfied with vague generalities about customs and landscape: he wanted information about the social life of the people in Egypt. As I had lived as a workman, manufacturer, and merchant in that country, he wanted me to tell him the precise extent to which the fellaheen were exploited by the Jews, the Greeks, and the English intruders; also about the usurious banks in Cairo and Alexandria. I was able to tell him how I had made iron-bound wooden chests for the Ottoman Bank, for the shipment of gold sovereigns overseas; and, when the Anglo-Egyptian Bank sumptuously renewed its premises, opposite the Bourse in Rue Sherif Pasha, how I had supplied the desks of red mahogany at a price of £60 each. I was not competent to discourse with him about "High Finance," which he inveighed against, as he said it was the cause of all the wars in the world.

We met frequently that year, as Pound was traveling to and fro between Rome and Rapallo. I have a vivid memory of what proved to be his last departure. I went along with him to the station. We found the barrier already closed, and the train beginning to move off. Pound lost no time in farewells. Taking a firm grip on the handle of his typewriter with his left hand, he took a flying leap over the barrier and jumped onto the moving train with all the ability of an American cowboy who vaults onto the back of a fleeing horse.

I never saw him again. But from the confinement of the prison camp near Pisa a treasured message reached me that recalled to mind the red mahogany of the desks of that bank in Egypt: a color that will always be linked in my memory with the bond of sympathy that was formed between us at the moment of our first encounter.

Enrico Pea

MOSCARDINO

The Signora Pellegrina went into mourning at once, she put on black silk, put a black hem on her nightgowns, lowered the blinds, and lit a lamp on the wide linen-cupboard.

She was of high lineage and had come in for the shares of two sisters who had gone into convents and passed away early, but her husband had been a poor hand at guiding the domestic economy and had left little either of her good heritage or of his own. He had been honorary physician to the Confraternity of the Misericordia, and High Chamberlain of the Church of San Lorenzo; he had had, therefore, a magnificent funeral.

The Signora Pellegrina showed no signs of grief at his passing. She said: Well out of it; you are.

Then she assembled her three sons and called Cleofe, the general servant who had come from the mountains, to act as witness:

You are all three grown men.

Your progenitors are no longer. Divide what is left.

The clothes I have on are my own. Don't grumble if I wear silk.

After that she forgot to talk, as if turned mute.

My grandfather was the youngest of the Signora's three sons. The middle one was named Lorenzo after the town's patron saint and also because he had been born in the year that the doctor had been made High Chamberlain (or accountant) of the Church of San Lorenzo. He had been sickly from the start, didn't walk till he was five, stuttered a little, and his remarks were so peculiar that people thought he was making up fairy tales. His father had intended him for the priesthood. That was another reason for calling him Lorenzo after the saint and the church with the marble steps and stone bench against its façade, and the chairs tilted against the outer wall from where one can watch the river with the winter sun beating down on poor men's bent shoulders.

Be it said that these oldsters were lined up like culprits with a cane gripped between their knees, and that they mumble without moving their lips so that they shan't make a draft or displace the air with their thin bodies. Noon stirs them and they carry off as much sun as has sunk into them, walking quickly because the shade of the acacias is full of pitfalls for age, and the acacias, lined up before the old folk's home, throw a shade even in winter, and steal thereby that much sun from the aged.

I don't remember the eldest brother's name but he had a terror of blood, he was grumpy and ugly and watched himself perpetually in the mirror, terrified and bursting into tears at the slightest provocation.

Servants did not stay long. It was not an easy house for a servant.

The Doctor and Signora Pellegrina used to get up for mass at sunrise and for communion. The girl was expected to tell Mrs. Pellegrina not to swallow water while she was washing, she was expected to hand the doctor the grey shawl that he wore like a cape over his shoulders.

If the boys had committed a misdemeanor they were expected to confess after mass, especially if it had been of an embarrassing nature.

Grumpy had his coffee in bed. He stared up fixedly at the servant girl, from foot to head with his knees hunched up to his chest and his horse face unshaved. The girl approached him with a feeling of terror and loathing, and Grumpy continued to keep his hands under the covers as if there was nothing in front of him holding a cup. Which nothing finally said: Hurry up! Signor Padrone. Whereafter he would at leisure bring out a hairy paw like an ape's.

The abbé wandered about the house all day long with his hands in the folds of his soutane. The servant was expected to say: Don Lorenzo, take your hands out of the slits. Then Don Lorenzo sniggered; went into the kitchen, lifted the lids of the pots with the ugly hands that had been in the slits of his soutane.

In the evenings when the abbé was in bed, the girl was expected to patch up the facings.

As my grandfather could not stand the click-clack of heels at certain times of the day the girl had to walk on tip-toe. He loathed seeing the abbé slinking about like a shadow. Every now and again he would rush at him, grab his long hair, pull out a few hairs from back-centre: O.K. that's where you'll be having your tonsure. He also picked on Grumpy, but less often.

He also slapped the servant. He was a devil when he got into a temper, upset the whole house, tore the bedspreads with his teeth, and if his terrorized family locked a door on him he would jump out a window.

The servants came, and left when they got their month's wages.

Cleofe, the last of them all, came from the hills with her bundle on her head, and my grandfather opened the door for her.

Good morning, Sir. She said it with such charm that he was moved. Cleofe blushed.

My grandfather in his bedroom listened for the tap of her heels, it seemed like a leit-motif, life in that house's monotony: click, tac!

Cleofe came from the hills by Terrinca, a place known for its beautiful women. They are long in the legs, with waists square as their shoulders. They are lean, with rather long faces, that seem perhaps a bit longer because they part their hair in the middle and coil it in two braids over their ears. They have very white skin, perhaps from the milk and flour diet. Their teeth are good, their lips full like those of young children, and their eyes are dark as the chestnut rind.

They carry baskets on their heads, old style, and take steps long as a man's. Their cheeks dimple in smiling. Cleofe was of this breed. It seemed as if no cloud had ever passed over that clear face and no tear ever had clouded her eyes.

How could she sleep hearing someone on tip-toe in the corridor, breathing hard at the key-hole?

How could she have stood it long, in anxiety, her heart thumping and a lump in her throat?

Poor devil from the hills, she felt that no such high love was for her, she avoided it, tried to be hard, and felt anchored to the spot when he looked at her.

"I will go. I will go." Another day passed and my grandfather's face, imperious as a general's, was there saying: Never. You can not.

My grandfather was in pain if she went into Grumpy's bedroom or when the abbé kept his hands in his soutane slits in her presence.

Don Lorenzo take your hands out of your pockets. She blushed if my grandfather was there to hear her. He saw it and trembled.

"I will pluck you like a dead capon!" He would have killed him but for Cleofe's intervention. She calmed him, patting his cheek.

Then my grandfather was taken with a mad passion and Cleofe could no longer meet his eyes without changing colour. Cleofe, do you like me?

Nothing was said for the rest of that night, in that house.

And yet everyone again heard the death rattle that they had heard a few days before when the doctor had got suddenly worse, and had almost sent for the confessor.

The rooms were full of ghostly population as that night when the dead man was no longer there but seemed to come through every opened door visibly, and a voice from purgatory seemed to move lamenting in the room.

And now the Signora Pellegrina hearing the creak of Cleofe's door was terrified as she had been *that* night. And rattled her rosary and kept listening as if he had come back from purgatory and was asking relief for his soul.

Grumpy sat with his eyes popping out the whole night, with his knees bunched up to his chest, in a bloody vision. He saw the war of '48 and the Austrian armies marching through the city, a high tide of fire, the forest moving, women disemboweled, children trodden into the mud by the horses with barbarian riders and the deafening noise of steel weapons.

Monstrous tale, my grandfather had told on his return.

He saw him in uniform, at eighteen, my grandfather who had planted the liberty tree in the town square, who had run away, who had gone venturing over the world, who had forded rivers, endured marches, killed enemies, plunging a bayonet into their kidneys.

My grandfather had upset an Austrian catafalque and slept in the dead man's coffin.

My grandfather scared him, made him tremble, made the house shake; what would he do now to the servant, to his mother, to Grumpy himself, to the abbé?

The abbé perambulated up and down in the corridor. Stopped at Cleofe's door, stayed fixed like a shadow with his hands in his pockets, with his head between the door and the door-frame.

The women of Terrina go to bed as God made 'em, naked.

Our house had no curtains, and the rooms are not dark at night. Don Lorenzo saw her naked, white, white, with her legs long. My grandfather seemed like a monster crouched over her, clamped to her belly, looking into her eyes.

The abbé stood there till the dead came to life, ill augured witness of my mother's procreation.

Cleofe, do you like me?

A' you? replied Cleofe bashfully as if asking it of herself, Do you like me?

That was after she got over her terror, and she had not cried out, feeling resistance was useless, and even if she had wanted to, had not the strength to cry out. Love had pinned down her arms, annulled and made useless the strength of her strong body. Her breath so caught in her lungs that she had no breath, and could make no movement of denial.

Cleofe found herself in his arms as a bird willingly in the mouth of a serpent, forgetting its possession of wings. Neither wanted to weep nor could help it.

Cleofe, do you like me?

A' you?

He was calm now, and looked into her tobacco-coloured eyes, held her head firm with his two hands on her cheeks and felt the blood beat in her temples, felt it in the pads of his fingertips, felt the warm breath coming from Cleofe's mouth that his hands distorted. Cleofe had the sea's tempest in her ears, felt the wind bringing winter now, over the house roof, in the tops of the trees that guard it.

In the courtyard was the well-curb with twisted ironwork over it, and the stone edge gone mossy, the cord looped over a hook, the well bucket hooped with iron shrunk on as a wheel-rim.

The well went a hundred yards down. Town perched on a mountain, the well, bored through clay and rock, narrow and crooked, down, down, through the cracks, through the tufts of nettle and pellatory.

When they drew water, the pulley wheel turned: Chio, kao, kao. The drops of the well bucket, coming up jerkily, echoed the clink.

Grumpy stopped his ears because the *gi-gi* of the pulley set his teeth on edge as sour lemon or when he heard pumice scraped on the marble sink. But since he was now domiciled in the courtyard he was drawn on by the curiosity to look into the well, drawn by the clear clink of the pulley that was like a bell struck by the subterranean spirits, so, little by little, with one ear, then with both he could stand hearing the turn of the pulley without feeling gooseflesh.

He looked down the well trembling and saw only darkness, not even water which the spirits had covered with lead, with a cloud-coloured mantle that was passing over the sky.

Grumpy thought he saw a river churning down there at the well-bottom, and thought he could hear a noise like that of the mill-race when the motive wheel moves in a sawmill. But he saw only a slab of lead and heard only the wandering of his own voice losing itself in the void beneath him.

When he grew bolder he threw stones into the well and saw circles shake on the water and saw his face in frightened reflection, deformed and recomposed in the whirlpool, submerged in the ripples as little by little the spirits restrained the water under their leaden mantles.

He began to take his meals on the green well-curb, casting a glance now and then into the deep at the swarming of shadows heaped like clouds, but smaller, a comic dwarf leaning there on his elbows the better to hide.

And he began to wind the well cord over the hook and the well crane, a hundred yards of it, bendable but shriveled stiff like a steel wire.

Grumpy made a regular skein round and united as the circles of the well water, smiling now and again. Thus he learned to look pleasant.

The abbé preferred to dawdle about under the orange trees which were also there in the courtyard aligned at the far end, clipped low so that the branches should not spread over the wall. If he looked down the well it made him dizzy, things swam before his eyes, he got pin-wheels as when he shut them facing the sun to see lights and glows of many colours.

There were the stubs of column, also, on which the old people had set the broken tubs from Montelupo that the tinker had patched up with wire and lumps of plaster, so that they now held earth as well as they had once held the washing. The old tubs from Montelupo with two masks and mottoes:

"Like to like."

"God makes 'em, and then gives 'em mates they deserve." Now they were full of rich earth, geraniums and daisies green in them so as to look like a shrub trunk with small flowers round it not passing the edge. Grumpy drew up the water, the abbé carried it to the old jars from Montelupo. They were painted now to conceal their age, the cracks, the snubbed noses of the masks, covered with a sort of red chalk that you use to paint tiles in a bedroom. Thus when the abbé had drowned the flowers that didn't pass the tub's edge there was a bloody wreath round the tubs.

Grumpy wouldn't come near them for fear of that spilled blood on the ground, and the abbé never looked down the well for fear of dizziness.

That was their way of passing the time, as it was now impossible for them to stay indoors. My grandfather watched Grumpy's eyes, and the abbé's hands stuffed through the unfaced slits of his soutane.

If Grumpy so much as looked at Cleofe, dinner was off. Grumpy barricaded himself in his room and the abbé had no hair left where his tonsure should have been, it was now twice the size of most priests'; and Cleofe could no longer keep my grandfather calm. Her gentleness only drove him wild and made him crazy with jealousy.

"Your brother will kill you one day." And Grumpy shut his eyes and saw my grandfather in uniform with his eyes shining scarlet.

And "that woman's" sweetish voice crept into his ears, trembling as if with compassion, almost as if she were weeping, there were tears almost in her voice full of urgency.

Grumpy no longer had his mother to fondle him. Threats at his throat if he so much as cast an affectionate glance, he crept into the house like a sneak thief, felt like a burglar if caught, barricaded himself in his room to keep from being flayed alive; and "that woman" who came so often to the well, did she know it? Did she know, and was she afraid he would die soon?

She was perhaps his guardian angel that had watched over his childhood. A great wave of feeling swept over her that she could express only with her eyes closed, weeping: Your brother will kill you one of these days.

Grumpy shut his eyes: And you, Don Lorenzo, do you remember your mother, before she went off her head? Nobody would touch a hair of your head then.

And Don Lorenzo sniggered, as he did when Cleofe looked at him.

Grumpy was drawing up water, and that woman stood with her thighs close to him as if wanting to help him.

When the bucket was in reach she leant over the well-curb to take it, crushing her belly against the green stone so that her thighs seemed to hold up two antennae as the wooden braces hold up the country-side bridges.

Her breast lay heavy almost falling out of her linen dress gathered in at the neck like the tunic of a Madonna.

Grumpy looked at the freckles on her breasts; so near now he could see her heart-throbs. Her throat brushed his hand and he shut his eyes as if in terror, and if the odor of lavender, released from the fold of the linen blouse puffed out by the weight of her breasts, reached into his nostrils he closed his eyes terrified with his legs weak as if in a fit of malaria.

So they remained hung over the well-curb in abandon, Grumpy's head drawn like a weight toward the well-bottom among the shadowy spirits which took hold of the bushy hair of the reflected head and beat it against the head of the woman reflected, so that the images were melted together, one over the other, striking and melting together.

Now her mouth was against his ear saying strange words, dizziness in his soul as in the ripples on the water beneath him.

Grumpy remained stock still with his eyes closed, he felt her mouth move away from his ear and fastened to his nape; a circle of fire, a brand to leave lasting mark.

But Cleofe who had brought her milky and blood-tinted face from the mountains now had circles under her eyes and there was a waxen shadow on her clear face. The dark spots that had showed her pregnant had not left with the birth.

Her mouth was no longer cool, her lips were thin now. Only her eyes seemed larger.

Perhaps her thought ran: If I had married a shepherd in my own mountains, now I would be happy. She wept in the daytime, lamenting that she had not enough milk, as have the women of her own village, they have it so that they suckle the lambs. That is abundance.

If she had married a shepherd she would be free, all that milk, all those sons, all that sky and a will to singing . . .

And now instead, she was afraid of the man who was her husband in that shadowy house.

Why do you look at yourself in the glass?

You have combed your hair to look prettier.

Why do you want to look prettier?

If someone went by in the street, if anyone stood near a window in one of the neighboring houses, if someone knocked at the door to collect a bill or bring a message, there was a bloody row.

Everything was in turmoil and chaos in my grandfather's mind.

Cleofe did not answer, ever. She obeyed, she looked terrified. Her face was full of suspicion, like that of my grandfather's, unquiet.

He wanted her not to wash, so that she would be ugly; to leave her hair uncombed, to wear the country clothes that she had brought with her, out of date, of grey flannel, plowman's shoes, canvas aprons, fichus crossed on her breast.

That she should look badly, that she should dress like an old woman so that no one would look at her.

And even so my grandfather found her more beautiful, too beautiful. It was the majesty of her figure; unsuppressible by the clumsiness of old-fashioned clothes. Taking from her the grace of fashion, her beauty shone through as a joke, almost as a dream, as if she were a girl of past time.

Sometimes he wanted to feel he was right, tortured himself, helping her to put on her good clothes.

A new dress of shot silk, with a white front and a low lace collar.

He wanted her to put on the necklace of gold beads with a cross, and with her hair coiled round her cheeks and ears as when she had come down from the hills. Then he watched her move away, his eyes fixed on her as if in a vision, as something no longer his.

He wanted her to stand on the balcony so that the sunlight could play over her dress, so the gold beads could come to life, so that her face would seem again compound of milk and blood.

He forced himself to indifference before the serenity of that wax Madonna, leapt as it were of a sudden from among the rays of God to his balcony.

But if anyone passed and turned unexpectedly, if a shadow showed at a window of a house opposite, the spell broke and his being was shattered, trembling, brute jealousy leapt back with all its instincts, he slammed shut the window to shut out the sun's kindness, he tore the gold beads from Cleofe's neck, trampled them, tore the shot silk dress to tatters, tore it with his teeth, stripped it off her.

Cleofe grew worse.

The doctor came to the house and my grandfather had a new war within him, everything in him on fire, so that if he concealed his anguish it shone terribly through his eyes.

Cleofe wanted to get well again.

And the doctor's presence increased my grandfather's torment, drop by drop, a whirling torrent, that Cleofe felt with terror.

The doctor had looked at her breasts, had felt her belly, pressed his head between her shoulders to listen, and tapped her white body all over. Cleofe felt it would drive my grandfather off his head. She wanted all the while to get well.

Her heart beat so hard, her legs trembled, now and again she felt a wave of heat pass over her face.

She wanted at all costs to get well.

She got up too soon. It was mid-September, a month of nostalgia for Cleofe, busy time in the mountains, getting ready the logs for the chestnut drying, they would smoke early this year as it had hardly rained all the summer.

The chestnuts were beginning to ripen in their burrs. The burrs had grown big, the nuts were full and meaty. They'll be smoking 'em early this year.

She stood by the window. Below was an arbor with ripe grapes hanging to the lattices. The arbor stripped of leaves with the wire braces, with the fronds and tendrils still branching, the dead branches bent with the weight of grape clusters, the shoots sticking out at the top with unopened butts.

A September already cold, though fanned with scirocco, a few reddish clouds, rain's sheeplets feeding in grassless meadow.

Heaven calm, but unlit, a grey dampness pervading the house and a will to let the eyes close.

My grandfather held her up by the balustrade, and she looked down into the courtyard or gazed at the light gallop of far clouds going mountainward.

The square orange flowers that had given fragrance in springtime were now dark balls in the lighter leaves.

In the tubs from Montelupo the small flowers were drowned, the water sloshing to the brim was tinted with the red cinnabar brick paint. My grandfather drew her from the balcony into his arms, put his palms against her shoulders, rubbed the backs of her hands, stroked down her arms, her flanks, her legs down to her feet, and lamented: Cleofe, you are too lovely, you are what is driving me mad, my despair, lifelong despair. Cleofe, I shall have no peace, I shall have no peace as long as you are alive . . . and I am alive. Cleofe, death is good. Death is good.

Cleofe repeated: death, and turned her eyes away, and toward the child in its cradle; which, awakened by the noise, kicked and screamed. To die. My grandfather had a knife in his hands. Cleofe, I can't kill you.

He fell on the knife, slitting his belly.

The first person to reach the door was "that woman," who had kissed Grumpy by the well-curb.

Then the doctors who put my grandpa in a straight waistcoat and sewed up his stomach.

He was off his head and didn't notice he was being carried away.

When Sabina, the woman who had kissed Grumpy at the well-curb, came in and saw my grandfather with his stomach slit, twitching on the ground, she ran to call her padrone, Don Pietro, Pietro Galanti who lived next to us and whose house had two doors, one on the tiled street and the other giving onto the courtyard toward the well. The abbé Don Lorenzo walked behind Sabina bobbing along to catch up. He went up Don P.G.'s stairs while she was calling the priest, he fetched out the silver crucifix and the stole and the surplice and the box with the holy objects that was in the downstairs cupboard.

It was not the first time he had scurried to death beds with Don Pietro Galanti and these were the things necessary on such occasions.

Then he fixed Don Galanti's tunic from behind and helped him to get on with the job as if it were perfectly ordinary and in no way alarming even if the slit stomach belonged to his brother.

Don Lorenzo stood still before Cleofe, smiled, stared at her quite a while with his hands in the folds of his soutane, quite calmly. Now, at any rate the disemboweled was in the hands of all those doctors and could no longer jump on him and tweak the hairs out of his tonsure as he had done in times past.

If you want to see your brother before they take him away . . . He may die . . . up on that mountain near Lucca . . . tied up the way they have got him . . . all that way on a stretcher . . . Signora Pellegrina, I wouldn't like my presentiment to come true . . . wouldn't it be better for him to die here at home . . . at least he would go to the cemetery where his father . . . and where we all, anyhow.

Signora Pellegrina, you might at least say something or other to keep 'em from taking him away . . . You are his mother, I have done every . . . I have told 'em to let him die in peace in his bed.

There was a pool of blood on the floor.

How can a man live without blood? It's true, it's all God's will, but God's will could cure him in his own bed.

To die in his own bed . . .

The mayor says it can't be done.

I haven't been able even to give him the sacraments.

The Misericordia will be here . . . anyhow it's your business . . . come see him before they take him away and give him your benediction before they get him out of the door.

Mrs. Pellegrina trembled and stared into nothingness, rolled her eyes from the depth of her arm-chair . . . and didn't answer.

Her teeth clicked from time to time, and the beads of the rosary tapped one against another. And a fug in that room that hadn't been opened for months, a smell of oil wick and of mold, a feeling of death. That skeleton hardly moved by its trembling . . . hunched into wide-sided arm-chair in the darkness of the room.

When the Misericordia did come with the coffin and the two horses the whole village was on the brick sidewalk.

Toward evening. Cloudlets reddish and dark, hurrying in escape, in herds, from sea to hills. Those far off seemed like one cloud thinned out on a turquoise sky, more blackish than reddish.

The cold breeze stung the women's faces and they stopped their mouths with their yarn tippets keeping their hands under their aprons so that their bellies seemed to bulge out. They stood stock still looking at our house, close to the opposite wall like a frightened flock of pregnant and widowed witches.

Those two horses with traces and harness ends of yellow leather, brass buckles, bridles with square blinkers that almost boxed in the horses' noses to keep them from shying, and with tinklers on their heads to keep them from going to sleep, bits with two small bars of iron sticking out on each side of their mouths, from which the rope reins passed over their rumps between two oval rings set in the tiny saddle atop the belly-band, rings oval shaped like old-fashioned key tops.

One sorrel and one chestnut with their knees bundled in cloth, their tails bundled up, with their ears twitching against the shiny blinkers, that man with the embroidered hat with the four reins between the fingers of his heavy hands, high up, above the horses, with his whip-end touching the ground and the covering of the catafalque trailing behind, covered with oilcloth like an uneven warming pan; a terrifying apparition never described in the book of fears.

Meanwhile it was getting dark and this mechanism started toward the Lucca asylum down the steep brick-paved lane, the creaking breaks slowed the wheels . . . chi-chi-chieee . . . wailing of wounded crows in the tragic evening.

A window was thrown open and a living skeleton appeared. A howl and thud. The pregnant witches took their hand out from under their aprons as if to deliver themselves from an evil.

Mrs. Pellegrina had fallen on her back. Broken her skull, could not be given the sacraments.

Everybody in this damned house dies without being given the sacraments.

I adore thee in every instant, O living bread of heaven, O sacrament of the most high.

Tomorrow thou shalt be with God.

Say: Jesus, Joseph, Mary.

But the eyes were set and glassy. Don Pietro had held a lighted candle to her lips and the flame does not waver.

Sabina, tie a handkerchief under her chin so her mouth won't flop open.

The rosary is in her hand.

She is dressed in black silk, all you need do is to light another lamp and keep watch.

Grumpy still had that pool of blood before his eyes, and his head now wrapped in a woolen shawl.

He looked in the mirror but did not recognize himself, he has seen the bare skull of death inside his face.

He has opened his mouth to count his teeth feeling they will drop out of his violet-coloured gums one by one before long.

He has wrapped his head in the shawl to keep out sound, to keep out visions. But the dancing lights suddenly swelled, exploded. Fire, fire, they were burning into his brain and he could not open his eyes.

He heard that woman's voice in his ears, a gust of warm breath on his neck, her mouth as that day at the well . . . and a going and coming through the house.

Tomorrow thou shalt be with God.

He no more knew which throbbed worse, skull, heart or head, it seemed as if a wind were tearing the shawl from his shoulders.

A gust of wind, like a gust of wind, he felt two hands clutching his wrists, violently holding . . .

and that woman's voice . . .

Perhaps it is a snare of the devil, and the wind is blowing . . .

Tomorrow thou shalt be with God. Jesus, Mary, Joseph another fire burst amid the bright dancing spots.

And the wind pulling his shawl. His head was stunned, it gurgled, flopped, thick and foamy as if the picked bones of his skull were full of red wine-must.

Death was helping the wind tear his clothes off, must he flee naked?

They would think he was mad, like his brother . . . They would take him to the Lucca asylum, like his brother . . .

And another blood-puddle.

Now they have put a cold shirt on him, they are laying him out in his coffin, they are covering him with a linen sheet, cold, rough, damp-ish, as when you get into bed in winter after long weeks of wind off the North Mountain, where the sun never comes for three months at a time, and the caves are full of icicles dripping.

His legs ache. He will never be warm again.

Jesus, Joseph, Mary, O living bread of Heaven.

The voice of that woman attacked him, a warm gust of wind on his neck. He seemed to feel her mouth now on one ear, now on the other. He no longer sees red.

That woman has squirted drops of ink into his eyes, she has sucked out the beast that was gurgling inside him, there in his head that is now black and empty.

It is night now, the baby stops whimpering, Cleofe is rocking it; rock, beat, double tap the legs of the straw woven chair on the tiled floor with a dull tap.

Cleofe looked like the Mater Dolorosa with the child Jesus. Resigned, pallid, unweeping. Unwrapped the child which stopped whimpering.

The night leaned its hairy stomach against the windows, the panes were warm and opaque, beaded with sweat. The window frames showed white, and the divisions between the glass squares. Outside all black, everything black in the room. A single candle is not much to light a whole room. The blackness hides behind pieces of furniture and bulges out round the sides. The bed has leant its shore on the floor tiling, a wedge-shaped shadow which shows exaggeratedly wide and odd.

It is mussed with the mattresses rolled to the top, the green and red stripes are like furrows at night in a mountain field.

Sugar is being burnt in a pan, the air feels viscous and sticky. The smoke passes in front of the mirror of the wardrobe and seems as if it would go on a long way into the darkness. They have washed up the blood spots with salt and water. The candle ogles, flickers onto the damp still remaining there, there is a huge patch between the bed and the window as if someone had dropped a wine flask.

Cleofe's shadow appears and disappears on the wall with the child at breast. Were it still you would say it melted into the paleness of the wall so vague that it seems but to continue the things about it.

Greyness, rain without clatter.

The sky is hooded over as far as the sea, seemed held up like a canopy by the mountains that edge the horn of Seravezza.

The tapers of the Misericordia crowd in along the walk that is paved with thin bricks, a thick cloud of smoke a bit above hooded heads.

When they had got the coffin onto their shoulders, it looked like a burning bier on four pillars, black pillars, quenched with the rain and suffocated with a dark brown cloth with metal corn tassels at the four supports almost unraveled in yellow.

The coffin moved thus down the steep lane, and behind it Don Lorenzo bareheaded, and the women with the brass lanthorns. The smoke of the torches hung in the air, tarnished the window panes, crept into the house, sticky, resinous, heavy.

Don Lorenzo is now in front of the coffin and stares at his mother in her silk dress, with her hands crossed on her breast, shackled by justice forever, her head bound, her mouth closed, one eye just a bit open.

They lift her from the litter by cords.

She is stiff.

They box her up like a bit of merchandise, put a double turn of rope round the casket and lower her into the grave as into a ship's hole.

The ropes are pulled up. They must be used again. They scrape against the rim of the casket with a dull sound of fraying, like pulleys of a crane.

Don Lorenzo's shoes were laced crooked with twine with mud on the ends at the low knot, and caked round the edge of his soutane, black stockings and silver buckles. He felt the water dripping down his sides from his hair, his face wet with rain and tears.

The hole swallowed back the loose earth. It looks as if yeast were swelling it up; puffing it over the edges of a garden flowered with paper, cotton and wire.

Don Pietro Galanti, family guardian, took possession of the estate. A vineyard on Ripa Hill, two bits of wood at Giustagnana, a spur of hill whose sub-soil contained a hidden vein of marble, graded "White P." The hope of the family.

The surface was rented to a charcoal burner for the time being.

Four houses at Seravezza, an olive yard and a field at Bonazzera, three olive yards at Pozzi, four farms at Cugnìa di Querceta, two poplar plantations and seven meadows at Puntone, Stroscia, Ranocchiaio, and Cinquale.

A life allowance of four hundred dollars *(scudi)* a year to a "legitimate son who takes holy orders."

Inventory of furniture, kitchen copper and household linen.

All entrusted to Sabina, Don Pietro's servant who is surety for her and keeps the keys of the house.

Grumpy got better. Sleeps now and again with Sabina.

Cleofe weaned the baby, anointing her teats with bitter aloe.

Don Pietro was deaf, he was seventy-one with a few smooth grey hairs more or less oily hung over his ears and straggled over his low forehead with three serpentine wrinkles scarcely showing in the thin olive hide.

Prolix by nature, knobby of nose he shaved his dry face daily. On Fridays he distributed alms to the poor of his parish lined up according to the sexes right and left before his front door on the side toward the mountain where the sun never comes in winter.

Not far from the house the mountain sweats; smooth grottoes cut in under the cliff with fungus-covered crevices, the sweat freezes with incredible icicles at its edge, exuded tears formed into glass work, as if the high altar were inverted by conjury candles without flamelets but lit from inside with prodigious transparency.

If a few wooden goats had climbed onto those blackish cavities, a shepherd with a crook and a brigand's hat, it would have made a grottoed presepio to be boxed in behind glass.

Not until April when the rain is tepid and the hollow under the cliff is warmed by the sprouting moss and by other delights of God invisible to us do the fantastic candles wholly drop off and the shadows cease to play in magic luminosity.

In April after the brief rains, the sky clears, the incredible glass work melts from the hills, carrying rotten leaves with it, the grottoes are washed and retinted. The pebbles of the walks are yellowed with mud, the feet of the poor therewith splashed. The rope sandals have lost their heels and the soles worn to a frazzle from being used all the winter.

Don Pietro Galanti considered his poor, saw them as souls in purgatory that see God and remain in torment, half in joy half in sorrow.

Don Pietro's poor have their feet in the mud and wait to be unfamished by providence, the sky is clear and nightingales are making new nests, the peach trees reflower and the orange trees in the gardens of the rich are pearled with new white blossoms.

Don P.G. opened his door at ten A.M. every Friday. He pauses a moment on the threshold to make quite sure there are no infiltrations of poor from outside his parish limits.

Then he emerges with his cloth purse containing the chicken feed.

The men lift their hats, the women stretch out their hands, "God reward you in paradise" was the usual verbal manifestation of gratitude, when not augmented by other explanations, excuses, after the admonitions inseparable from the eleemosynary act.

Don P.G.'s gabble annoyed the women particularly and he was specially and nauseously longwinded with widows. He required peculiar religious observance and exemplary conduct from widows.

On Sunday Don Pietro said the ten o'clock mass and his poor flocked to the balustrade, otherwise no hand-out the following Friday.

He came slowly out of the sacristy so as to have time to count his poor. The altar boy meanwhile put the missal on the reading stand, set out the cruets of water and wine, and stood patiently at the foot of the altar steps chewing over joyously the next week's freedom consoling himself with the idea that the next week's longwindedness would fall on the junior clerk his companion.

Ten o'clock mass in San Lorenzo at the altar of the warrior saint Discoglio lasted an hour, invariably. That is until the start of the other mass said by Don Caesar, the other thin priest. Don Pietro's opposite in temperament and in habits.

Don Caesar sang out of tune, had no manners, loose-jointed as the sandy cat from the nun's pharmacy, he loped up the altar steps, his head moving on springs, his hooded eyes blinking against the candle light trying to find the rubrics in the missal, in fact rather like the royal blackbird in the Piazza butcher shop, pecking at the raw tripe which its owner stuffed through the wire bars of its cage.

Don Caesar thin, tobacco stained, choleric, bungling, liberal, untidy, boozy, impatient at the door of the sacristy, his legs nervous, and tapping his heels on the stone step near the bell tower, with his eye glued on the altar of the warrior saint Discoglio, awaited for Don P.C. to get to the Salveregina and leave room at the altar.

The little bell for Don Caesar's mass broke in without manners on the opening words of Don P.G.'s Salveregina, and shocked the sensibilities of Don Pietro who despite his deafness always heard the bell and felt as if it were a set of rude words addressed to him personally, and thought within himself of blasphemy and the sin of him who approacheth the altar fasting but with his heart full of wrath and presumption.

They passed midway before the High Altar, one with his eyes sparkling with hurry, the other lowering his so as not to look at him, and seeming to nod to each other as they both bent head and knee before the sacrament of the Most High.

Don Lorenzo, the abbé, was not an ordained priest and did not come in for the annuity.

He had been to the seminary before his father's death but had forgotten whatever scraps of Latin had been poked into his block. He had even forgotten the Paternoster and the Salveregina and when he served at mass he mumbled at random clucking in his throat like the women of the people when they try to join in the Latin litany.

He had been thrown out of the seminary for keeping his hands in the slits of his soutane. Up till then his father had been supplicant, had begged the Archbishop time and again to find some way to consecrate him so that he could get the annuity, after which he promised to shut him up in a monastery so that with patience and God's will he might then get a little sense and education.

If his father had lived he would have fixed it one way or another; he would have taught him to read the missal by ear and from memory; he would have had him anointed priest so that he could get the annuity.

Instead of which, he had been left to himself in the courtyard, under the orange trees, to count the buckets of water which Don P.G.'s servant pulled up to water the tubs from Montelupo, and finally forgot the inscriptions on them and the conception of the bottoms of his pockets; forgot that pockets have bottoms.

Don Pietro Galanti had to restart with the first exercises. He kept the house key and watched him by night. Lorenzo was put on rigid abbé's regime "rules for ecclesiastics" as Don Pietro called it, and had so impressed the abbé with this set of rules for ecclesiastics that he now kept his eyes on the clock for lessons and meals.

The house, watched by Don Pietro, took on new aspect. The abbé occasionally went to Cleofe's room, she was half the time in bed, half in the arm-chair. But he no longer smiled at her or kept his hands in his pockets; he stood mute and looked at her in terror as if my grandfather's shadow might at any instant appear.

Sometimes when Cleofe slept he was moved to tears, thinking of his mother nailed inside that box under the ground.

He felt Cleofe's death coming, because her breath came so gently, her eyes were sunk, her pallor.

Cleofe seeing him at her bedside so often and so changed, showed a maternal tenderness for him.

He blushed, began to shake again, and looked toward the door.

He felt a new attraction toward Cleofe, and thanks to this feeling he tried to look different. He had a sense of well-being, of self-respect, a sense of being alive, a sense of life, now, a bit late, just as he had learned to walk late.

He now seemed to see clear inside himself, he had new feelings never known before now. Setting his eyes forward toward death he seemed to see the limits of life, opening an unknown world, a hidden treasure.

Now he could even shed tears, not for his bodily aches and pains but for his soul in torment. So that, still seeing his mother's coffin being lowered into the grave, he was moved by Cleofe's lips sketching a smile for him.

What is life anyway if it be not softened by such tenderness for one another?

To feel that someone cares, as your own mother had, after your mother has gone under the earth.

To feel the desire to clasp the person loved, until she can no longer breathe, to be wholly united with her body. To take something eternal from her lips which can not be said with words. There it is. One could be happy in this world if the devil didn't take up arms against you.

He crossed himself, so that the devil shouldn't appear and blot out his reason.

Before summer came, the doctor ordered sea air for Cleofe during the spring and part of July . . . because she had suffered so much, passed a horrible winter always shut in her bedroom.

The days began to lengthen and Cleofe had been getting up for several weeks. She coughed less; but if she went down into the garden and walked up the stairs afterward she was weighed down with enervating weakness as if she had climbed a mountain. She broke into light sweat toward nightfall, her cheeks got red and at once a light sleep like a slight torpor obliged her to close her eyes and she would stay in a doze for hours.

It had been a stiff winter, the grottoes, the river's high banks, the ravines had been constantly frozen. The water in the ravines and rivers could be seen working along with difficulty under a thick plate of ice, seeming to suffer from want of air.

It must have been gurgling loudly, whirling strongly, because it shot up at the edge of the ice all foamy. The branches, thistles, dry leaves borne along in the torrents had been caught fast in the freeze, imprisoned as if asleep, like birds in a cage of water.

The wheels of the sawmills were ringed with short thick candles of ice, with filaments and drops like pin-wheels for the Madonna del Carmine, curious boughs and branchings were formed in the riverbeds as if half sculptor's fine marble, half mottle in the rough stone ways gouging the bottom. Even the horse turds and cow droppings were made fantastic and precious between the icy mud of the cart tracks.

So after the feast of St. Discoglio, new varnished by old Ciampino who was also church upholsterer and decorator, there reappeared after many years the fine old *giardiniera* wagon, six-seater all new black and yellow with the curtains of heavy linen fringed with blue.

Grumpy was bundled up, cocoon'd with a grey shawl round his neck, such as his father had used, more grouchy he had aged so much in so short a time that many people seeing him staggering into the wagon thought of his dad, not merely because of the shawl but from facial resemblance.

He stood beside Sabina who was in her new clothes with circular earrings and with a pink handkerchief over her head stuck on with a gold pin that looked like a nail rammed through the nape of her neck. Her face blazing, gesticulating and rolling her eyes and her hips shaking with the wobbling of the wagon. Vibrating with full contentment she alone in that vehicle felt, and was, boss, brazen, proud of feeling that she was the real boss of a six-seater with sky blue cushions covered with ticking that could carry so many people.

In town clothes the family doctor, bachelor, red-skinned, sat opposite Don Pietro Galanti who shot knifed glances stealthily at him when turning a leaf of his breviary.

Cleofe had the lowered curtain behind her serving as support and cushion to what was left of her saddened body.

And the abbé Don Lorenzo next to her with his little shiny eyes, tickled the baby's neck as it sat in Cleofe's lap.

———

Sabina and the red doctor were the live animals in that funeral coach. Their thought was clear, concealed by nothing save the conventions of the moment. She burning with the exuberance of healthy vitality, he a man of scant learning and no scruples whatever.

Their carnal eagerness was of a certainty visible to everyone. The others moused round the same question, of flesh in heat, with tortuous imagination, and turned in on themselves in their uneasiness.

Cleofe had her eyes on the frosted hills, on the olives shot with sunlight, which fled under her gaze as she was carried from them. She let herself be borne along as in a dream without thinking, as a soul in transmigration, as if her life were ending, gently, in beatitude, and the child which as yet had neither reason nor soul, slept cradled.

The red poppies amid the grain flashed into Grumpy's eyes. The red head of the medico jutted out like a flashing ball of copper, speckled now and again by rays of sun at play in the branches. Dizziness, dazzle, those splotches of sun leapt from the doctor's red poll onto Grumpy's hands and played over them, and onto his grey shawl, his face, and bit into him with a voluptuous malignity.

Grumpy felt the pain almost on the surface of his skin. He had been feeling pain ever since the doctor had asked to go with them and use the sixth free seat in the carry-all.

But as they went along this painful sensation grew more and more unbearable till he had to scratch his hands now and again as if stung by an insect, and tap his face now and again. He had to keep from looking at the doctor's head because he always met the watchful eyes so near him . . . as if they were right to strip Sabina stark naked.

And as they went along and along the doctor's eyes (Jack of Clubs) knew more and more about Sabina's legs, now that her dress, losing its laundered stiffness, stuck to them, now that there was a hollow between leg and leg made by the weight of Sabina's hands resting there.

And how would Grumpy have the courage to say a word of reproof to the doctor who could give him a powder of something and kill him off like a dog if he needed the doc for a constipation?

He worried: That doctor will come every day as he has done for two years . . .

And is today the first time? . . . and he convinced himself that the doctor had come to an agreement with Sabina, they had cooked up this trip to the seaside between 'em.

Jack of Clubs had arranged with her that he would be waiting by the new bridge under the plane trees.

Why had she told the driver to go by the New Bridge and not by the Annunziata?

Was it Sabina who told him? Cleofe's need of sea air had been invented on purpose?

This had all happened because of Cleofe. He hoped she would die soon and end it. That confounded consumptive would hang on for a long time yet, he would have to stand it or die off himself.

He scratched his head, his hands, got up, hitched the shawl round his neck, looked at Don Pietro Galanti with begging eyes. Turned his eyes to the fields, there were the red poppies. He looked at Cleofe, there was that damn one-lunger, cause of it all; who might at least die off and end it, then the doctor wouldn't come to the house any more. He didn't know where to look, if he cast his gaze inward he was terrified. He remembered all his past life, the meeting at the well, the first fear of those mocking reflections down in the water beneath him, which took him by the hair and slapped him against Sabina's face; that was the first bewitchment, hoodoo. Then that woman kissed him. That brought the blood of his disemboweled brother back before his eyes.

He saw red for the rest of the drive.

Gulls at rest on the sea-water, in little groups, crowds of them further off, others scattered over a sea fanned by a cool northwest wind. Patternless as a field of daisies sprouting in an unbounded meadow.

A sea paler than spring grass feathered by so gentle a breeze, petals blown off, deflowered.

A sea streaked by little furrows, unpatterned as soon as formed, as if a golden comb passed invisible, lining the white and blue, a page of the book eternally fabulous upsetting all men's calculations.

On the hard beach inshore the water scarcely moved, without foam, as if the sea breathed in blessed rest. No shadow of effort in the sleeping giant.

Cleofe hunched up on the sand under a black umbrella, not much shade, but enough for her. She does not feel the sun's heat though the sun is already high.

With all the pale sea in her eyes, sinuosity of the gulls, small pigeons new hatched, black and white with their wings open on the live water. Great lake as a bed for water lilies, amazed at the soon come summer.

Tota pulchra es. Wholly fair art thou, Mary full of Grace! The abbé Don Lorenzo was reading the book of Sunday prayers for the month of May the most amorous pages that the faithful can say to the Virgin when she stands in the silver niche unveiled for the evening novena, with the golden rosebuds and the celestial mantle and on her rosy forehead the crown of lilies which shines and shakes to the echo of children's voices.

Wholly fair art thou, Mary, *piena di grazia*, said the abbé in a tiny lowered voice in the shadow near Cleofe.

It was the first time he had been so near that Madonna, who seemed to breathe, absorbed, with all the gleaming sea reflected in her tobacco-coloured eyes.

That pale wax face, the head bent toward the left shoulder, protected from the sun rays by a black baldacchino, with the child at breast as Mary in the desert of Egypt, followed by Herod. Eyes the colour of Macaboy snuff.

Full of grace; wholly fair art thou, Mary; for the first time Don Lorenzo dared to speak so near to her, protected by the shadow of the little black rain umbrella.

Tota pulchra es, Mary, *piena di grazia*. He spoke the words of the Christian poet, and though protected by the shadow he was not free, he felt his heart caught in his throat and coughed every now and again a dry nervous cough.

He laboured and mistook the words, and the accents of the prayers which he would have liked to sing out in a song for her, to her, who watched the sea and listened to the break of the wavelets like the rustling of starched petticoats.

Don Lorenzo's words were heard, perhaps, and carried away by the angels who form the crown of mortal praises about Maria Regina. They were absorbed in space as if they had not been uttered aloud.

And in all the circumambience there was a divine and placid agitation of love, a submissive labour, a weeping without sobs, a smiling without disturbance of men, or of things, a calm striving.

The men scratching for mussels in shore with iron pincers stood like the gold hunters in dime novels silently prying off shellfish amid the sieve of sand that the water left alternately dry; sousing in it the motherly water, bitter, pungent with the salt rinsing, then popped it into the wallets slung over their shoulders. Washerwomen came only to the river because sea water doesn't wash clothes, baskets on head, full of the white week's washing, planting their poles in the sand, stretching their ropes with sure wrist, they fold the big double bed sheets and the spreads covered with white heavy hookstitch.

The swaddling bands turned three times round the wash lines are gayer than the brides' night gowns with crossed lace. These last if the wind bellied them out seemed stuffed full of decrepit flesh. More amorous the towels with fringes like corn-ears with red mottoes and names interlaced in the corners. The smaller bits are baby blue like the hills of Seravezza after sunset.

All this festooned wash moved a little, as the sea by the beach, as the wings of the gulls, as the mussel fishers, as Cleofe's bosom, as the voice of Don Lorenzo, as the passion of the red-faced doctor and Sabina's carnal response, as the suspicion of Don Pietro Galanti and the churning of curses held in by the cowardice of a taciturn husband.

You have sewed me up with black thread, Don Pietro. You have sewed me to your tunic, like a rag button. Black thread don't show on black cloth, no one will see the stitches. But it is fate that I am your servant, even now that I am married. Wait, wait, serve always. Nobody ever waits on me, ever has waited on me.

First I had a job with an old priest in a house with no light, a dark house, now I am servant to a priest who has grown old, even older, and a young priest, and instead of a husband who has the sense to agree with me, I have one who agrees with my boss, if you call it agreeing when he sulks, hides in a corner, lengthens his mug; rolls his eyes as he does when you tell him what you think, Don Pietro.

I was evidently meant to stay bundled up in black thread and mend long black socks worn out heel and toe by priests, sew on black rag buttons, patch soutanes, mend pockets, brush the nap of priest's hats, and their hat cords and bat-wings. And if I go out for a walk and to breathe a breath of clean air with healthy people, first you jump on me, then my husband, and finally Don Lorenzo as if I was married to all of you three.

Life is a black thread bobbin, we live by needlefuls. But God measures the measure. I am seventy-one, Sabina. I think my life is at its last loop.

You can already see the white on the top of my wooden poll.

Don't be in a hurry, don't curse your servitude. Bear with my old age as I bore with your infancy.

I wish you would think of me as your father, if priests could have children. I brought you up, you may say, with pap and pacifier, and when you were grown I gave you good housing. If you no longer like me, I have been deceived by your benevolence, have you lost the good Christian qualities that I taught you?

What do you mean by "your servant even now that I am married"? You got married, does that mean that you are to kick over the traces and run wild like a yearling in heat?

If you do, you aren't like your mother of blessed memory. And in saying this Don P.G. got excited. He lost that serenity so habitual to him even in difficult moments.

And Sabina listened to him with irritation as if champing on the bit of a discipline grown insupportable.

The wind turned icy and harsh, the sea roughened and cast off the gulls as if impatient at having tolerated their perching on its rump for so many hours.

The calkers prophesied rain from the heavy flag-like clouds that saddened the heaven. There will be a downpour of big drops before long, pocking the sand waste.

They stretch brown oilskins over the upturned boats, awning'd out a bit further so they can work under them as under a cabin roof. The men looked like journeymen sweeps and locksmiths in orgasm, who on arriving in a country square when it is about to rain find the peasants asking sweeps and tinkers, have they brought the rain and bad luck? Then they look cross and don't have their chimneys done or their kettles fixed, if it rains before the tinkers' tents are up and the forges and bellows got going.

The calkers push aside ropes and nets, get astride the boats on the part plugged already and calked, and start again tapping the chisels that enlarge the cracks to get out the old tow between plank and plank.

The pitch smoke from the boiling iron cauldrons spreads out low, hanging heavy in the clogging heavy air, hiding the little hunch-back half naked who tends the fire and blows.

I lived with my gran'dad on Monte di Ripa.

My mother worked in the city. My father was dead and I had a brother who had convulsions, who stayed with a woman who looked after him out of charity. That woman was the butcher's wife and helped in the butcher shop and to kill in the slaughterhouse.

On slaughter days she didn't come home and my brother was alone shut up in the house, and he had convulsions.

They sometimes found him on the floor, as if dead. Sometimes she got drunk and cursed, and beat him.

At Carnival he died, and that woman said: blessed paradise!

She had been to the Carnival dance, and came in and stepped on him, then she noticed him. Took the cold body and threw it onto the bed. She took off his checked suit and spread a sheet over my brother whose soul was now safe.

I didn't see him, but I know what he looked like. Once I had seen him twitching on the floor, the door was half open, and the woman who kept him out of charity was at the butcher shop, and I looked through the key-hole and called him.

Then I ran to call her, and when she came back he was stiff.

I didn't see him dead but I can always see him stiff, as he was that day.

My gran'pop, called back to his native earth, called by the house and the town, had come from his travels to stop on in peace.

All his life had been voyage from a dream to a dream, from township to township or to far country.

In his young days the war had taken him as volunteer into its toils. Later, love armed his hand again. But neither love nor war had absorbed him. Now he felt the blood less restive in his veins and less turbid in warming his heart.

Middle high, live glance, biblical beard like my own, thick hair shining like filed iron. Face bright and rosy, thick mulatto's lips like a sucking infant's, he talked of life and death; of Dante, love, early grain crops, manures; half shutting and wide opening his eyes as if fixing an image when he got het up over poetry and things of that sort.

If, on the other hand, he talked of his own past life, of Cleofe, of the mad house, of the way gooks carry on — and he had passed the best part of his life among 'em — his voice grew gentle, he explained things as if he were talking of someone else.

He had the same intonation when he talked of Aladdin lost in the magician's cave among the jewels.

Every now and again he would try to fix a lost detail.

He laughed over his wasted life. It seemed to me odd that he would get into a passion when he talked of the Emperor of Hell with three heads of hideous colour so big he could eat a sinner in each of his three mouths at once. What excited my terrified fancy were the six black wings on the shoulders of so huge an animal, stuck fast to his midriff in ice.

As I had heard that many people sell their souls to the devil to get money in this world, I shook with fear at night, when I thought that my grandpop in some need or other in those far countries might have sold his soul to the devil.

Once he told me that when he was a kid and on the point of drowning he had seen the Madonna.

That made me cry.

We were at the hearth and it was raining. My grandfather had put out the light for economy. The room was lit by the embers. I was on the hearth with the Pomeranian bitch. My grandfather on the straw-plaited stool. I hid my teary face in the bitch's yellow coat.

My granddad began to mutter through his teeth, then roared at me: Take down that dog! Put down that dog!

I set the dog on the wooden floor. My granddad got up suddenly, opened the door and drove out the dog. That is the way to bring up cowards, instead of men. If I don't die too soon I'll learn ye!

Shut up the stable! Go feed the sheep! He opened the door. The water groaning in the gutters splashed on my bare head.

Foscolo was a small-sized black dog with rather long thin legs, pointed ears and a tail sticking up.

Our next-door neighbor who was older than granddad and as crotchety had taught Foscolo to walk on his hind feet, to bring back stones, to hunt for a hidden handkerchief, to eat raw onions, to drink wine and hold a lighted pipe in his teeth.

Our next and wrathy neighbor came in the evenings to sit at our fire, with a gun slung over his shoulder, with Foscolo as lictor.

The old men got het up and talked of happenings, and I rolled about with the two dogs scraping round on the floor in the dark in the next room.

That sole distraction, I waited for with infantile joy.

Those two dogs were my world.

I was convinced that they knew me by name, I noticed that certain yaps were my name, namely BUCK.

They called me "Buck" by those yelps as I called them by their names.

When Foscolo was tied up by the neighbor's threshing floor, I called him: "Foscolo." He replied with a long howl always the same, so that I knew he was tied. If on the other hand he was loose, he barked pleasantly, jumping around his old master as if asking permissions. Then I knew he was loose and continued to call him. Sometimes he did not ask permission. He came quickly through the vines, made four capers and rushed away.

Even my granddad was fond of Foscolo, because he said our Pomeranian bitch had lost her virtue and was no longer any good as a watch dog, since the time she had been carried off with the carts that carry the wine down to the plain of Lucca.

If you give me Foscolo, I'll give you the bitch. Pomeranians are scarce in these parts, and I'll give you a rooster that's a phenomenon, they've promised to bring me from Apulia. It's a cock without claws.

It don't scratch. You can leave it loose during seeding time. Eggs that cock makes will be wanted, you can sell 'em high everywhere.

The old neighbor laughed in his face, with his pipe wobbling in his mouth, betting that that clawless rooster was a hoax which my educated granddad wanted to put over him a poor old contadino.

One evening my grandfather said to our neighbor: It won't be more than a month before Foscolo's stopping here and I bet you won't be able to drag him away even if you chain him and try to.

"Baa' guum, I wanna see thaat." And he kept Foscolo on leash from thence forward.

My yellow bitch began to dance and prance about Foscolo who also got playful. But the blondine raced off, into the shrubs, and came back sidling up and sniffing and moving off with odd movements such as I had observed in unbroken colts.

Catch me if you can, she seemed to say to her fiancé, who looked at her with infantile patience as engaged lovers who play at having secrets and excuse the capriciousness and coaxings as if happy to be more childish than they actually are,

to reduce themselves to greater weakness despite their having double the strength of the weak female,

they come to playing blind man's buff

in the hedge like butterflies, like the blondine Pomeranian and Foscolo.

My grandfather sent me to call our neighbor and when we got back the fiancés were already married, behind a rosebush.

There you are, old cock, right there in the bed where the violets bloom in April.

But now it is winter and the hummock is green and the rosebush is a bundle of thorns.

But do you think those dry twigs haven't love sap under the ground? Do you think they haven't subterranean witnesses to their amours, like us watching Foscolo and his blondine?

And do you think this grass — fur hasn't an amorous hook — up under the ground?

You will see, after their pregnancy, their sons will be born, thick on the hills as sand in a riverbed. Believe me, old sock, we are the ugliest of the lot. We are all dogs of one breed or another.

Foscolo was now standing quiet, almost asleep with his black muzzle on the yellow Pom's neck.

That's it, Buck, that's how your father begot you. And that's how you'll beget yours when you're married.

We are all dogs of one sort or another. It's a shame to talk like that to a kid nine years old, said the peasant.

Tell him with cleaner words, you old bugger, if you can find 'em. How did you come into this world?

And now take away Foscolo and keep him on chain.

Foscolo is no more use now.

Nothing is holy save the field where he has planted his seed, for continuity, or if you like, for immortality.

If we were talking of Buck's seed I would say immortality. Man is made in God's image; and one should burn incense to him.

The old neighbor looked bewildered and scandalized. He looked at me, and moved his shut fist over his mouth, lifted his elbow to ask if granddad was drunk.

I shook my head.

He shut his mouth. Opened his eyes extra wide. Shrugged his shoulders and went off full of suspicion taking Foscolo with him, tied with his leather belt.

Grandpop picked up the bitch and said: Now we must treat her respectfully.

The Apuleian cock was a common and very scrawny rooster with bare scaly legs of egg yellow.

He hadn't even the strut of a cock that serves many hens. He was a bastard little cock who would have become a deballed and crestless capon if my grandfather hadn't bought him from his original peasant owner.

Nothing good about him except his white feathers.

There was a sudden shower the day granddad bought him. The rooster with his legs tied had been chucked on the ground in the shed where we took shelter and had got his wings and belly covered with mud.

When we got home we washed him with water and soap, and so that he shouldn't get dirty again, we put him in a barrel to dry, and in the dark to keep him from crowing.

The downpour had made wash-outs along the banks of the boundary lane and my grandfather noticed that the break was all stones badly piled up, round stones, chunks with no corners such as you find in furrows of fields not before plowed, and that the peasants call field bones.

Grandpop had been going up that border drive for a long time looking at one thing and another, remembering what had been when he was a boy and went to the vineyard to get in the grapes. He got into a row with the old neighbor about a big fig tree which he had seen when new planted and which seemed to him to be too far on the other side of the boundary line.

Now the wash-out showed how the boundary line had been shifted. Granddad began to hum, stroking his beard, when he saw the neighbor coming along a bit thoughtful, saying that the bank was of no importance and that he would see to mending it himself.

Grandpop pretended not to understand and said: Tomorrow that Apuleian rooster will be here.

The neighbor grinned: Hey! by gob, I'll bet you three flasks of old wine . . .

Late that evening when we were sure the neighbor wouldn't come over that night, grandpop went down to the cellar, took the rooster out of the barrel, put it in a bag and brought it to the house.

He took a pair of pinchers, lit the lamp and said: You remember, Buck, when you were at Querceta, one of the farmer's hens always came into the house? Yes. And when I grabbed it, I said to you: If you speak I'll do you in as I do this hen? Yes. And I cut its head off, and we ate it that night. We put the feathers in a sack and the bones and went and buried 'em a long way from the house? Yes.

All right, Buck, now I tell you: If you speak, I'll pull out your nails, as I propose to pull 'em out of this Apuleian rooster.

I held the cock in the bag, with its feet sticking out; I felt it shake and shudder; and my heart beat and trembled as if I were committing a crime. The cock inside the bag was braced against the table, and the pinchers gripped its claws and used the edge of the table as fulcrum, and you could see the claws come out from the pulp like little teeth from a kid's jaws; and a spurt of black blood came out from he flesh.

Granddad had put on his glasses.

Every now and again he would look into my pallid face. He seemed to enjoy the operation.

When the eight claws were lined up on the table like eight bits of confetti, he heaved a sigh of satisfaction. He put down the tweezers and heated some oil. He anointed the feet of the Apuleian rooster, bound 'em up with bits of rag and took the bird back to the barrel.

The neighbor hadn't been easy and trusting for quite a while and no longer came in of an evening.

He had to be asked several times to come look at the rooster.

He brought Foscolo on lead, and I greeted my friend Foscolo and ran to get the Pom for a frolic as usual.

But the dogs seemed almost unacquainted; they hardly said a word to each other, a few mere civilities. I attributed this coldness to Foscolo's iron chain and the neighbor's having tied him to the leg of the table. Foscolo tied up like an assassin felt the humiliation.

The neighbor felt the rooster to see if it was made of real meat, pulled its anemic wattles, touched its crest with curiosity. There was reddish skin in place of claws which made him think it would grow its claws late.

The rooster walked on the table, slowly, very slowly, gingerly, as if its toes hurt.

Sure! It's a friek!

It's not a friek, it's a BREED! thundered my granddad, and the argument started.

When the old bloke was at the end of his arguments he decided sadly to go get the wine.

It started off as a joke.

Even Foscolo drank a glass of wine. I drank one. Foscolo danced on his hind legs, had a pull at the old man's pipe; then went to sleep under the table because the show was getting dramatic.

The old bloke got drunker, then he was afraid of my granddad, thought the scrawny Apuleian cock was a devil. He found the devil's claws in the last glass of wine and was terrified.

He wouldn't believe they were the claws of a mere cock born of a hen.

And my grandfather grinned at him: Look how that rooster is laughin', he's laughin' at you. He's got an eye on you. He's lookin' at you with only one eye.

The cock was hunched up behind the lamp by the wall.

Every now and again he opened an eye at the sound of grandpop's voice.

Look how he's lookin' at you!

See how red his eye is.

There'll be claws to wake you in hell, you damn thief!

Perhaps you'll turn into a crazy rooster, and the devil will send you to play jokes on old thieves, as this cock's played one on you.

See how red his eye is, going round and round, his eyes are still burnin' with hell fire.

The poor old buffer began to weep.

He made the sign of the cross, then got furious. He reached for his gun and it wasn't there. My granddfather had hidden it first. Then he began to shake, and his teeth rattled as if he had caught a chill.

Then gran'pop started a devilish conversation with the rooster. He asked questions in a foreign language, and answered in a different voice.

He paid no attention to the old peasant who begged for mercy, trembling before him and the rooster.

I'm goin' to die. I wanna confess. I don't wanna be damned. Intercede for me Mr. Rooster.

And he clasped his hands before the cock, and finally got down on his knees on the floor.

Then gran'pop put a chair near him and put the rooster on it and then said: I am the Holy Ghost. Confess! Confess!

My granddad was right. The fig tree was too far from the boundary. For fifty years our neighbor had taken the stones which came up with digging and plowing, and carried them to the boundary, and thus his land had spread over a yard and a half all along the edge. His property had been cleared, fondled from one end to the other.

In his vineyard the wine was now better because the old buzzard has shaken up the earth, taken out stones, taken out the bad vines, rooted up strawberry grapes and planted columbine and aleatico grapes.

Now the Christian labourer was old and about to die. He was leaving a perfect vineyard to his family and was receiving from God the reward of his labours, the sight of the Apuleian holy ghost to whom he could confess his sins before getting ready to pass on . . . a divine favor.

That's what my grandpop told him, and took him home late when the jag began to wear off.

On the way back we stopped near the fig tree. Grandpop paced off the distance to the boundary. I looked at the moon low over the sea. I saw the Ligurian hills and the roofs of the towns in the plain.

Two gun shots, one right after the other.

And the rattle of shot in the frosty grass between my bare feet, like the points of poison thorn, made me jump gasping: The old boy has shot himself!

No! he wanted to shoot us.

And granddad started down the boundary lane, talking of the frost that was bad for the vine shoots.

We passed the rest of that winter alone, granddad and I in the evenings with the light out.

I on the hearth stone, and grandpop on the straw stool, by the fire, the brand was of luminous olive wood and gave a lot of cinders and very little flame.

Long boring evenings ending with yawns so steady as to make young Buck weep, despite his being all ears and alert to hear the true fairy tales of his grandpop, illustrated by examples, coloured with pictures of clear poetry and somber drama; telling how the lunatics with whom he had lived twenty-four years fell in love with the new moon. They prepared curious wreaths of flowers for her, without leaves, five or seven kinds with the same number of unspotted petals, a real certosian and geometric field, studied and worked out lovingly with a smile on their lips, their eyes bright and absorbed.

And there are other nice lunatics so gentle they can call the birds with names you have never heard. Until they see birds in the sky, fabulous, all made of air, invisible and transparent. Others talked with the wind and with field flowers. Or they praised God from year's end to year's end, standing still in a corner with their eyes turned up to heaven and their arms folded.

Others have no use for talk, tongue doesn't work, they would stand mute for ages, guarding what secrets?

But if the lunatics had cut open their bellies for love . . . Or others, in sleep, stabbed with crazy jealousy had strangled those whom they ought to have loved all their lives, and now wept because they were dead, reappeared to them in sleep . . . They saw them upright, steady, still in the garden cross-walk, waiting till they could get out of that prison to be reunited and go on to heaven knows where . . .

Generous, impatient outbursts of that blond young fellow, all eyes and sinews of steel, jammed into a straitjacket near my grandfather's bed in the first days: Near the big window . . .

He saw her, he leapt up to go to her, and she always turned off toward the shrubbery and didn't see him. And didn't see his chained love, and he was tied up by his rival who wanted to steal her from him . . .

But who couldn't because now he had written to the queen, and she will come with coach and footmen and maid servants to free him.

But in the meanwhile *she* has turned off by the myrtles and don't know this. Let the queen come and she will fix it O.K.

It grows dark and *she* is still there by the standing still.

Perhaps she is chained and don't hear, and don't see her lover behind the barred window, in pain, crying out, and making signs. But he can't call her by name because her name is made up of letters that aren't in the alphabet any longer.

And the women that so terrified me in my grandfather's stories, women turned into mooing buffaloes in bestial conjunctions in the marshes of the maremma. I can still see them going on all fours prodded on by pock-marked guardians in white overalls.

And the others that tear off their clothes without knowing why, and have lost all shame and talk excitedly with the men without suspicion of sex, and at night roll up in the moonlight like hedgehogs in underbrush.

Violent men that had killed many kings of the earth so that mankind might be sated with goods, who support your chains with pride, and shake every now and again and tug at the straps that bind you. To run again to your place of combat in the world, shoving it along with mighty heaves so that it will revolve more quickly. Beautiful and terrible your bloody fury! How many times have you slept with me on my cot, with the few coverlets in those long winter nights.

Don't kill me. I am not a king's son.

And I would wake up and think of the sons of kings born with such cruel destinies. One does not know why God puts so heavy a burden on their shoulders.

And those women huddled weeping on the ground from morning till evening.

Undone, because they have forgotten, lost something they can not find again.

And they bend over, opening their eyes wide and full of tears. These lanterns lit on a rainy night, to hunt in the corners, in the cracks of the pavement, in the chinks of the wall.

They have lost something. What have they lost? They wander about sobbing like marmosets, souls in purgatory paying their sins, seventy years for each lie.

And look at the doctors with eyes half shut, leering at the other women of whom they are jealous. They walk along scraping the walls, with little short steps so as not to be seen and recognized; and all day and every day with their hands tied, because if the doctor unties them, they will begin to scratch their mons veneris till the blood comes, as if they had a herd of lice there at pasture.

This was the son of a Luchese emigrant.

He had lost his reason in an American forest, and lost his way home. He made friends with the apes in the forest, eating nuts and wild fruit. He slept in the trees for fear of snakes, he became a thin ape with long nails and a hairy face. But carnivorous teeth wanted meat. Therefore in bad weather he ate the carcasses killed and left by the other wild animals.

He was found by relatives, peasants near the forest. Recognized, captured, like a wild animal he tried to bite them, refused food, let out guttural howls like a lion.

Thus he was brought back to his native country, and my grandfather knew him in the days of his adventure.

I followed him step by step on his return voyage. He followed, he began to call his father, then he remembered his smallest sister.

He learned to smile. When the doctor pricked him with a needle he felt it. And man is man on condition that he feels pain always in two ways; that he feels grief for a distant family, and pricks on live cured flesh.

His cure was rapid. He got well before my granddad, so that he became his nurse and consoler.

My grandfather despaired of getting well, getting over the flow of madness that every now and again centupled his strength and drove him to devastation.

After the cure of the Luchese emigrant, he understood that he too would get well.

You must want to get well, said the Luchese with kind words, when my grandfather lost hope.

Unless they want to, nobody will ever get well.

Thus he had to want to get well, use his will to get well. And my grandfather began to want nothing except to get well.

Not that the Luchese emigrant was dirty, quite the contrary, but this was because it was more beautiful to be clean than dirty; not because dirtiness makes men ill. On that point no one could shake him. He didn't believe in contagion and laughed at the doctor's meticulous hygiene.

Eleven million microbes can get onto the sticky side of a postage stamp.

Alive? interrupted the Luchese emigrant, looking clever.

Alive enough to bump you off in a very few hours. But can eleven million living creatures that I can stick onto the end of my thumb be that powerful and invisible all at once?

That was something the Luchese couldn't understand. Sometimes he thought the medicoes had heard this hocus-pocus from the lunatics.

When peculiarities mentioned in the story were shared by one of our acquaintance, my grandfather would say: "A drop or two more or less will make the jug slop over; another drop and the jug will slop over.

That chap would be a nuisance or dangerous. And his relatives or someone would put him on a closed wagon and cart him off to the gook house up there past Monte Quiesa, and down the Sercio valley and then up that little hill, and shut him there in the sanctuary, where he'd have a much better time.

No one is totally sane.

No one is totally crazy, it's a matter of balance, measured in the interests of the half crazy who decide about their half sane fellow men.

How often have I heard: He's a good chap, but just a bit enthusiastic.

Or: he goes off at full moon.

That's his weak point, don't try that on him.

He's got a bit of smoke in his top story, gets all het up over nothing.

He lies like a trooper, always digging up something."

"Watch 'em when they get drunk, give 'em an extra drop and they get so kindly, kindly, so kindly.

Laugh like hell and roar like the devil.

Can't stand up, and blame it on the earth's goin' round. Another one will grab a knife and think everyone's against him.

Have you ever seen drunks start pissing and dumping like beasts in front of everyone else?"

"It's a matter of degree.

The richer can go further than poor folks.

In every rich family there are at least two, if there are four in the family, who would get shut up in the sanctuary of Frigonaria but their parents, mostly doctors with stinking sores, put up with 'em and excuse 'em, and say: Little horsey will stop when he's run himself tired.

In the meantime rich folk's crazy children go on squandering what their parents have welched out of poor lunatics.

There is a law of compensation even in this:

See my house.

And he came back: Pleasant to sleep in April.

April's way comes down barrel a day.

Grumpy, Don Lorenzo and Cleofe. The red-faced doctor, Sabina, Don Pietro Galanti in the wagon, in the spring, coming back to the village."

Those are the names of the lunatics. Grumpy. And now Don Lorenzo. Cleofe's fever came back, the pain, the sleeplessness, the enervating sweats. She went back to bed for a week, seriously ill.

Then she got better.

And thus it went on till October, when the streets of Seravezza rustle with leaves and thistles, blown down from the mountain with the first frisky wind.

Again appears Grumpy with his head bundled up, with his ear glued to key-holes, listening for the doctor's voice and Sabina's, who no longer slept in his bed:

She had had a girl child that looked like the red-faced doctor, with red hair and a freckly face.

If he got ill there was that doc, Jack of Clubs at the door: won't die of that, takes more than that to kill 'em.

Or he ordered a medicine which Grumpy didn't take because it might have poison in it.

The veins swelled on his neck, he got red as a peperone.

There was no doubt of it, the red head persecuted him. Jack of Clubs came and said they should bleed him.

Grumpy was scared and objected. He knew that his time had come. Jack of Clubs wanted to kill him and get Sabina, who was now his whore and had had a child by him, which Grumpy couldn't bear to touch.

He felt aversion for blood not his own. He couldn't stand that reddish fuzz and the scabs on the top of its head.

Even Don Pietro Galanti couldn't get a word out of him.

Nothing for it but to recommend him to God.

Jack of Clubs said he ought to go amuse himself for a month in a city to get rid of his hypochondria, and Grumpy knew it was just to get him out of the house.

The Doc said: Even Lucca. And Grumpy knew the gook house was in Lucca, where his poor brother was.

But you got to get over this mania, said the Doc. And Grumpy cowered down under the bedclothes, waiting to be copped.

He heard 'em saying the one lunger was no worse and that she was getting better, and Grumpy knew that he was the one who was going to die, that Jack of Clubs needed to keep Cleofe alive in order to be able to drop in at any time.

With Cleofe as an excuse he could come in and enjoy Sabina and see his maggoty brat.

And he, Grumpy, couldn't say anything, for fear of those shiny scalpels that the doc had in his leather case.

One of those little knives could make a little hole in his skull and the blood would come out a drop at a time, and even those few drops were a sea without port or harbour.

He thought he might kill Cleofe.

She was so full of t.b. she would die sometime sooner or later. But he wouldn't have had the courage to die.

He thought of arguing it out with the abbé, might find some complicated way to convince him; the abbé could do it, always in Cleofe's bedroom.

But when he opened his mouth to start explaining to the abbé, with the long argument that he had been chewing over for days, and masticating inside his groggy head-piece, Don Pietro Galanti appeared at the door.

Grumpy felt his tongue swell up between his teeth, and he couldn't get his mouth shut again.

He locked himself in his room.

He remembered his mother, dead without the sacraments and with one eye open.

Believe in God's punishment!

He hung himself with the cord they used to hang out the maggoty brat's dirty diapers.

"I never wanted to ask how Cleofe died.

She must have faded out bit by bit with solemn humility:

Without useless sighs.

Without wasting a breath, must have closed her snuff-coloured eyes.

Don Pietro Galanti probably said to the red-faced doctor: It's a pleasure when they die that way, just little by little.

At least there is time for the sacraments; neither too soon nor too late. And get to heaven before other sins can get onto their soul . . ."

"I heard she was dead, years later, when they thought I was cured."

"The nuns brought me your mother in the Campana Institute uniform. I knew like a shot, and made a sign that they shouldn't say anything; for the pity I felt seeing the child in those ridiculous clothes."

Printed by The Stinehour Press
in Lunenburg, Vermont on 60 lb Mohawk Vellum paper.
Designed by David Bullen Design.